Solospaceman Modern Love

Table of Contents

Chapters

1. Contents
2. Solospaceman Image
3. Fix It
4. White Love/Nobody Likes Me/Omar Ming
5. My Date with Cicely Spears (Pages 5-9)
6. Going to College (Pages 10-12)
7. My Date with Nicole (Pages 13-14)
8. Drawing/Notepad/Final Copy (Pages 16-26)

Note: Attaching your interpretations of each story creates a story's chapter! Begin your interpretation of each Solospaceman story at the end of each Solospaceman story. Then continue it in the Drawing and/or Notepad/Final Copy section found at the end of this book.

Silencer

Watch Silencer Animated T.V. Series on website: solospaceman

SOLO SPACEMAN
SOLO

Modern Love

Fix It

In my house, it was 12 midnight or at least the time of darkness. Therefore, I could hear and see unfamiliar sights and sounds such as heavy raindrops falling outside on the ground and on top of my bedroom's windowpane. In a dark and similar manner, I heard and saw water dropping from the ceiling of my living room to one of its window ledges in my living room by my lamp outside of my bedroom's door. That made me afraid of getting out of my bed and moving around my house to fix those paranormal occurrences.

Compared to the many other nights of me sleeping peacefully in my bed, this night and its Daja vue caused my psychokinesis abilities to move objects in my head anywhere, at any time, over and over again, up and down, and all around and around. So, I began to wonder what was happening to me. Then I thought to myself... then I asked myself... where is my betrothed... where is my beloved... where is she... where is she... where is the ghost of my first love?

Then I saw her standing on the top of my staircase, while I looked down at her form the elevation of my bedroom's door. There she faded in and out disappearing more and more each time she grew more ghostly gray. So, in order to keep her from totally vanishing, I bumped into her at the same time her head and arms were extended and moving in my direction. She responded to my actions by saying, "Fix it!"

White Love

I would like to say
That there was a day
I dear to dream the dream of White Love
But like an apple that has rotten
My love seems to have been forgotten
And my White Love was thrown away

Nobody Likes Me

I was at a party where all the lights were dim. For some reason, while I was noticing the low lights, I began to feel that nobody at the party liked me. So, I tried to shake my feelings off by attempting to convince myself that they were all in my head, but when a very pretty young lady who was handing out rulers stared right into my face, did not give me a ruler, then handed her rulers out to everyone else at the party, I knew that my feelings were justified.

Omar Ming

On a mountain
On top of its peak
When we are lonely
We will go to weep

We'll look over trees
And far beyond the coast of any sea
There valleys are filled with flowers
But we will waste away the hours
Weeping you and me

While in the green green grass of home
You and I will still roam
And pray to God that we find
Within each other peace of mind

My Date with Cicely Spears

My Date with Cicely Spears was not a traditional one. In fact, it came about only after I had researched on my computer websites which featured new modern dating methods. That is, in the old way of dating, it was not unusual for a man to ask a lady that he had known for many, many years several times to go out on a date with him. If and when she finally agreed, then the man would be responsible for all of the date's arrangements such as its financial expense. Also, when they went out, they followed strict dating rules such as no kissing or sex on the first date.

Today, modern online dating is pretty much the total opposite of traditional dating in that two total complete strangers might hook-up online by using a computer website dating service which allows them to introduce themselves online as well as exchange demographical information there without being in the presence of each other. Also, women ask men for dates, the time spent on the date may vary, and date expenses are usually shared if not totally paid for by the woman.

Keeping up with the times, I not only met Cicely Spears online, but also made arrangements with her for our first date... there. On our first date, we went everywhere we could go, because she kept repeating to me, "I can only spend a short amount of time with you." So, on our first date, she did everything in her power to make our date a memorable and pleasant experience for me. In fact, her diligence in keeping the most intricate details of our date in order was so appealing to me that she reminded me of Princess Lea a dating specialist.

Anyway, at one point on our date and after we had visited the Eiffel Tower, we rode down a long escalator. Then, as we rode it back up, it became a more and more joyful experience for us, because we both realized that we were falling in love. Also, other in love couples as well as other potential in love couples as well as estranged people boarded the escalator as we were rode it up. By the time we had all reached the top of the escalator, there were enormous crowds of various people everywhere. When they saw us together, they stopped what they were doing and started to stare at Cicely and me. It seemed as if they were all waiting for us to hold each other's hands or to engaged in a long and dramatic kiss, but we did neither. And, shortly after that our date ended.

Oh, by the way… before I continue my story, I would like to mention, when Cicely kept repeating that she could only spend a short amount of time with me, I responded to her declaration by asking her these few questions, "Am I psychic… or do I have extrasensory perception… am I capable of precognition or retro-cognition, magical thinking or mind reading?

After she did not answer me, then I said to her… …because I know what is going to happen to you. I saw it happen to a lady on T.V.. That is, for several decades a certain aristocratic woman dreamed of purchasing a particular large and beautiful greenhouse which in her mind was located on the outskirts of the southernmost tip of a small French town. In fact, night after night she saw the house within her dreams in such vivid and colorful imagery that she began to believe that it was a real place *but* not a real place.

Fortunately for her and quite by accident, she discovered that it was a real house; because one day as she was walking home from church she saw the house standing erect on top of a tiny hill just around the corner from where she currently lived. So, she bought the house thinking that she was fulfilling one of her most ambitious dreams. Sadly though, after she had purchased the house and lived in it for a substantial amount of time, she fell behind in her mortgage payments. Then she was evicted by the house's rightful owner along with all of her Earthly possessions and thrown into the streets of her small isolated valley.

Cicely, you may ask, "Why did you tell me her story?" Well, if you did ask me that question, then I would answer you by saying that it reminded me of an experience I once had within the confines of my own home ownership. That is, I remember… I was in my new first floor apartment on twenty third street in New York City's Upper Eastside. It was a huge place. In fact, it had a large glass front door like that of a department store's front door and directly on the opposite side of it, it had another large glass door which lead to the rear of my new first floor apartment and outside.

One day, out of curiosity, I stepped outside of my new apartment's backdoor to look around my new backyard. It also was a large place. In fact, it was so large that it had a car parking lot in it. While I stood there admiring it, I noticed that some neighborhood kids were playing basketball in it. So, I stopped what I was doing in order to reintroduce myself to one or two of them. Then one of them and I began to walk and talk along the side of the basketball court, until we found ourselves walking up a flight of short stairs. There I saw before he did all sorts of drug paraphernalia scattered everywhere on top of the short stairs' flat deck. I tried on at least 3 different occasions to clean up the mess, but when I saw in a corner of the parking lot a mod of angry Arabs yelling, shouting, and protecting American politics while holding explosive oil cans in their hands; I decided to abort my mission, said good by to my friend, and then left the basketball court.

 Afterwards, because I had nothing to do, I proceeded to walk to my old middle school to get a chartered bus to go on a one-day trip. As I boarded the bus, I noticed a very pretty girl named Brittney that I wanted to meet sitting in the rear of the bus. She sat there as if she was looking for or waiting for someone else to come. So, I turned for a second to pay the bus driver my fare to ride the bus. Then… I looked in her direction again. To my surprise, this time instead of noticing Brittney, I saw a military funeral precession which consisted of about ten marines marching behind the window where she was sitting. So, I sat down beside her and asked her if she knew anything about the deceased person. She answered, "No!" Then we reached our bus stop, we got off the bus, and went our separate ways. Although it was not much of a romantic randevu, I did enjoy speaking to Brittney on the bus.

 Nevertheless, my one-day trip was to what I thought was an obscure park that I saw advertised in the bus's traveling brochure just before I decided to take the one-day trip and got onto the bus to do it. Still, when we reached our destination, I went into a building in the park in order to change my dirty and sweaty cloths; because it was an extremely hot summer day and my wool business suit and Eskimo shoes made me feel very, very uncomfortable in that day's heat.

Anyway, as I was changing, I looked out of the room I was in and its building's first floor window. With that glance, I began to recognize that the park I was in was Prospect Park where I went to school as a child. So, I made sure that I was as quiet as possible, because I also came to realize that the name of the building I was in was Mount Sebastian Hospital. It was a hospital for the elderly. And, one of my older sisters worked there.

In the room I was changing in and while I was still changing, I started to hear people walking and talking and coming in my direction. So, I tried to hide from them, because I did not want them to see me naked. However, my fears of the approaching strangers began to dissipate, once I realize that it was a clean-up women and a male nurse who were coming my way. When they reached me, I explained to them why I was there. Then the male nurse called me by my first and last name. I was shocked that he knew my name. But, later, I calmed down, after he explained to me that he recognized me as his son's fifth grade elementary school teacher.

Then out of curiosity I looked into a nearby closet. There I saw a picture of me. Then more pictures of one of my older sisters and me. I was amazed by them, but knew that I had to immediately leave the hospital before my older sister that was in the pictures with me knew that I was there instead of at work. So, I considered the fastest way to reach Springfield. The bus I used to get to Prospect Park traveled too slow, and I needed a faster type of transportation to get back to work before my big sister called to see if I was there or not. So, I decided to take a cab to get me to Springfield.

As I entered the cab to get to Springfield, I hoped that the cab driver was not a drunk driver who speeds his passengers to their destinations. Because, unlike me who one day was driving at the speed of a ghost rider... drunk... cabbies should never drive drunk. Here why, on that day I was speed racing by myself in my car with no other cars around me, I had a drink in my hand. All of a sudden, the glass and the rum inside of it started to travel out of my hand at a much greater speed than the rest of my body and car was moving. In other words, the rum filled glass of liquor fell out of my shaking hand and started to spill its liquor all around my car, because I was drunk.

This is how it happened! As it and I turned the archway of the highway that I was driving on, my drink on its own accord accelerated out of my hand at such a fast speed that I could see it in mid-air as it moved away from the rest of my body, out of the window, and traveled far, far away from my car and me. It and I stopped, when we reached a stack of horizontal dead dry human bones that were lying piled up one on top of the other on the other side of a street's intersection red stop light we had reached. The bones got there because the night before I had reached the intersection there was a terrible storm that cause them to fall there from the graveyard situated directly above the intersection and its lights.

Needless to say, because of that incident (seeing dry bones) when I returned home, I was traumatized. Then I decided to go to sleep. As I slept, I heard someone or something knocking at my front door and then entering into my living room. He… she, or it tap me on my head, which woke me up and brought me back to the reality of our world. Then it stole from my living room and me my most prized possession. It was my star-fire-rim-stone computer tablet. Then he… she, or it walked back out of my room, through my front door, and out of my house with it. Cicely, that paranormal experience is why I told you this narrative. It relates to you in that you were supposed to learn from its many stories within a single story not to trust strangers as I did when I walked into my new apartment's backyard, took a one day trip, and went out on a date with you… Cicely Spears.

Going to College

Going to college can either be frighten, dreadful, or an awe-inspiring experienced event. The question is how one determines which category best fits the decision that he or she made to attend college. Well, one way to establish the correct answer to that question is for the person who decided to attend college to answer more college related questions. For example, he or she might ask themselves… Why am I attending college what is in it for me… then… Am I going to college to learn a trade… a profession… or to socialize and make new friends… What are my learning objectives… What are my learning strengths and weaknesses… How do my learning strengths and weaknesses affect my specific learning goals… What should I major in… Do I have the necessary prerequisite course work to enroll in the major I am considering… How do I choose the best college to attend that corresponds to my prospective major… How long will it take me to earn a degree… More important, do I need financial aid and if I do need it, then where will I get it from, when will I need it, and how much of it will I need?

As a loving uncle, I had to address one of my nephew's concerns about him attending college. So, after asking him to consider his answers to some of the above college related questions, I drove him around our small town in my old and dirty beat-up jalopy, until we had came to Montgomery Berkheimer University which is an "old school" well established educational institution. There, as we got out of my car, people stopped and stared at him, because of his physical disability. That is, he has muscular dystrophy.

Nevertheless, he was impressed with the campus of the college especially after I had explained to him some of its history. So, he went inside of its main building to find out more about it. After he had obtained several flyers, pamphlets, and brochures from the main building's information desk that better explained Berkheimer University's college life, we traveled around the campus sightseeing looking for specific places on campus that were high-lighted in the flyers, pamphlets, and brochures, until we came to its swimming pool where he rolled his wheelchair up the wheelchair access ramp in order to go inside of the swimming pool building and get a better look at its swimming pool. I guess he wanted to see if it was or was not handicap accessible.

At any rate, once I saw that he was safely inside of the swimming pool building, I decided to sit down on one of its many outside public benches, rest for a while, and wait for him to return form the swimming pool area. They say that a flicker in time is worth a dime. So, in order for me to constructively pass this particular moment in our college sightseeing expedition, I started looking into the pool building around the pool area through its many large opened windows and admiring some of its beautiful avant-garde architectural attractions.

When I looked up at one particular section of the pool, I was able to see that it was designated for women's swimming. Then, first, I saw one gorgeous young female model in a bathing suit swaggering her hind parts from left to right as she walked directly in front of me. Then I saw two gorgeous young female models in bathing suits swaggering their hind parts from left to right as they quickly ran pass me in order to Jack Knife dive into the twenty-one-foot-deep section of the Berkheimer University's swimming pool. Then I saw an uncountable number of gorgeous young female models in bathing suits all studding their stuff around the swimming pool's deck area seemingly without any concern for who or what may be watching them as they frolicked around in it.

Puzzled by their appearances at such a prestigious college as Montgomery Berkheimer, I shook off our unexpected encounter as just another extraordinary example of how quickly our turbulent times cause social change to take place in even our most highly respected conservative institutions.
In fact, because I am a product of the Obama Era, I really was shocked to see how liberally those lovely female models openly participated in seductive games at such a conventional collegiate establishment as Berkheimer University especially when I remembered that during the 1960's Berkheimer was one of the few colleges in the United States not to conform to participants of the Hippie Movement request for students to attend its college without uniforms. Also, during the same era, it refused to stop its students from publicly praying in school before they attended their classes. And, of course, Berkheimer University did not allow segregation to permeate its facilities at any time in its long school history. So, again, I was completely baffled to see how openly in public the young female models at Berkheimer University's swimming pool were displaying their accesses as they frolicked around in it.

        Irregardless of those facts, after firsthand witnessing the cultural and social changes taking place at Berkheimer University, I, myself, decided to apply to attend the college even though that particular decision was completely contradictory to my conservative ways of thinking and made me somewhat of a hypocrite in the eyes of my young nephew. So, because I am a Vietnam Era Vet, I went to the Veterans Administration office at Berkheimer University and explained to one of its many counselors my intentions concerning attending her school. She needed a break from her daily office routine, so we decided to meet inside of the Berkheimer University's main cafeteria. There she told me as we enjoyed our lunch that if I wanted to attend her college, then I would have to mail her the college application that she was handing me by placing a small picture of me on its light green see through envelope. I agreed to do it then reunited with my nephew to explain to him that after answering several college related questions, driving to and around Berkheimer University, sigh-seeing on its campus, and witnessing the social changes that are taking place there, I have decided that we are both going to college.

My Date With Nicole

After rambling about my date with Cicely Spears and providing you with details of it, I am going to tell you about a girl that I dated, after I had dated Cicely Spears. Her name is Nicole. In particular, my last date with Nicole was totally unlike the first date that I had with Cicely Spears. In fact, you may find it difficult to follow the sequence of events in it as well as the logic to it, especially after you hear what happened on our date and the consequences of those events by reading about them and judging for yourself the accuracy of the above statements. And so...

My last date with Nicole started with us sliding off of a slippery slope. Why? Because, when I picked her up for it, the very first thing that she said to me was... "The hunch that you had about my job situation was more than a gut feeling... because my boss did fire me. Consequently, I did lose my job. It turns out that he did know about us and our candescent meetings. Apparently, he had videotaped us on several occasions as we dined, went for a walk, and simply enjoyed life instead of being at work. He showed me that he had captured those events by displaying them on a very large flat screen T.V. inside of his office, after he had called me into it for a private meeting."

I responded to Nicole's grumbling about her job lost by asking her these few questions, "How do you think that I knew you would unequivalently lose your job... I guessed... precognition... retro-cognition... daja vue... magical thinking or... collectively... none of the above?" When she did not answer me, then I said to her... ...because... yes... it is true... I did know that your boss was going to fire you just like I also now know what is going to happen to you in the future, because in addition to the original premonition that I had about you, last night, I had another premonition about you that once again showed me your future. In fact, I saw a very similar thing happen to another anxious young woman many years ago. It involved her falling into a deep, dark, and Black Love.

Nicole: A Black Love?

Narrator: Yes, a Black Love!

Nicole: What happened to the lady who fell into a deep Black Love?

Narrator: She threw it away.

Nicole: How did she throw it away?

Narrator: She made the ultimate sacrifice of it by finding a new and different person to love other than the original Blackman that she claimed to be so in love with in the first place.

Nicole: Oh, of course, you think that is what is going to happen to us.

Narrator: Yes!

Drawing and/or Notepad

Please place your drawing and/or written interpretation of this story here!

____

Continue…

Final Copy

Drawing and/or Notepad

Please place your drawing and/or written interpretation of this story here!

Continue…

Final Copy

Drawing and/or Notepad

Please place your drawing and/or written interpretation of this story here!

____

Continue…

Final Copy

____